Mr. Whole=Sum

Enchilada

By

Bryan Billingsley

Dedication

- To my earth angel, Daniel

- You are my Whole=Sum

Daddy

Acknowledgments

I would like to thank God first and foremost. My family Stacey and Daniel Billingsley. My Parents for all their support! And my friend Pancho Stevens. Dreams can come true when you are pure of heart ❤️ 💙

A special thanks to Megan Barr for the help in editing this book.

About the Author

Bryan Billingsley is originally from the "Show Me" state of Missouri. He was raised in the north county suburbs of St. Louis.

After completing his two bachelor degrees, one in Exercise Science and another in Physical Education at the University of Missouri, Bryan began teaching Elementary Physical Education and coaching High School Soccer in Naples, Florida. Continuing his education completing a Master's of Physical Education from the University of South Florida.

He is married to his high school sweetheart, and they have one Mr. Whole=Sum Enchilada and a boxer dog named Dempsey.

Sharing a passion for teaching and fitness, this book creates an educational tool for pre-K and elementary students.

What are the parts that make up this extraordinary Mr. Whole=Sum Enchilada, you may ask? Let's count together to find the Whole=Sum!

One, he is second to none!

Mr. Whole=Sum is extremely loved! Truly, deeply and unconditionally! Too much isn't possible. Never too much!

#1

Two, wow look at you!

Mr. Whole=Sum is growing so fast! He wakes up to the most important meal of the day. His parents know he needs a healthy breakfast and proper diet to grow strong, think clearly, and feel energized all day.

#2

3=

Three, a cardinal flies from the tree.

Mr. Whole=Sum starts each day happy with a positive attitude and smiling face. He takes a minute to appreciate nature and tries to be nice to everyone he meets! He has always been taught "it's nice to be nice."

3+0

2+1

1+2

#3

4=

Four, shut the front door!

Mr. Whole=Sum lives an extremely active lifestyle. He loves to play outside and participate in sports with his fellow enchiladas. It is a known fact that he loves soccer and would play all day, every day if he could. It is important to find an activity that you enjoy regularly.

4+0   3+1

2+2   1+3

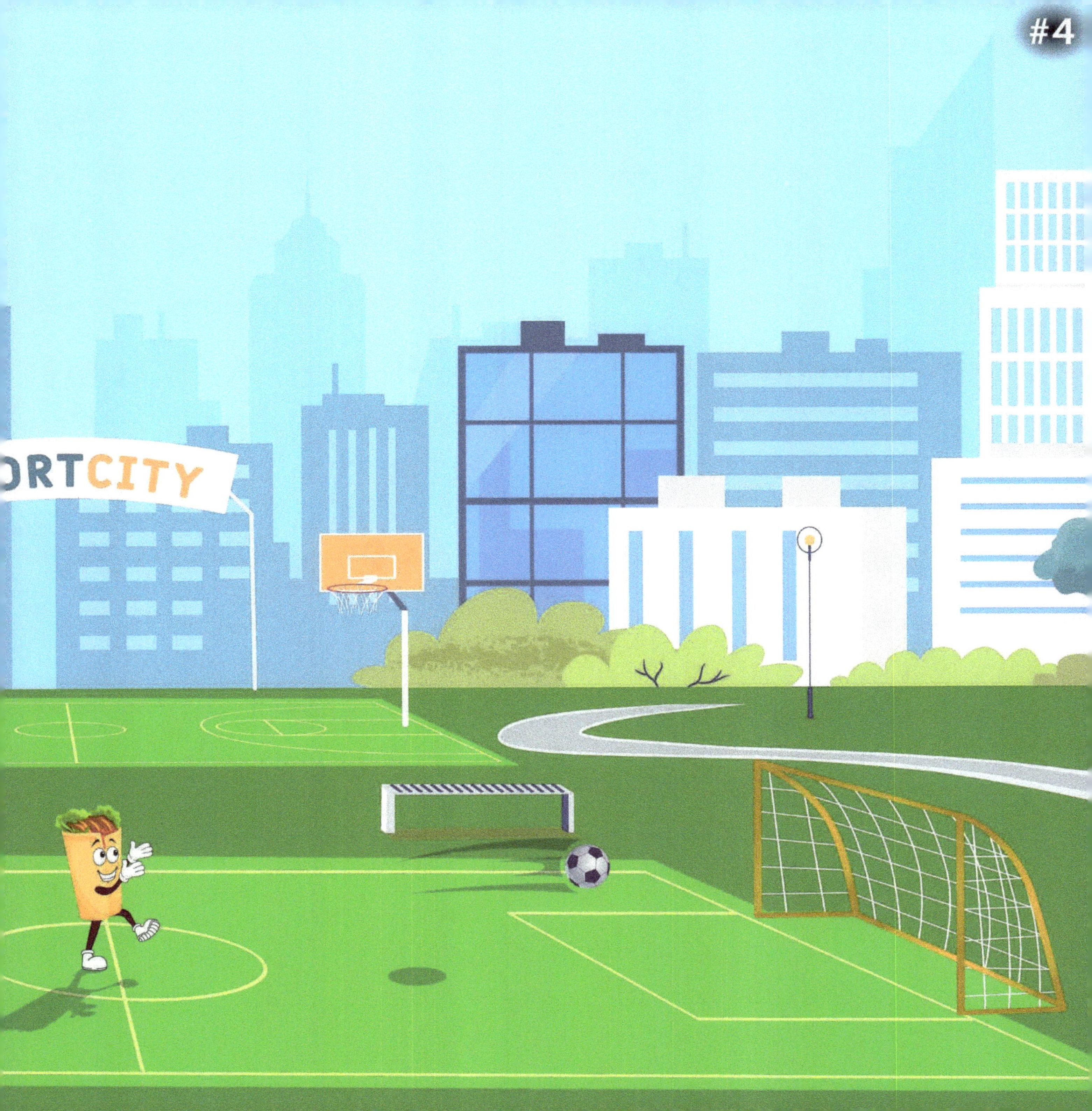
ORTCITY

5=

Five, and feeling alive!

Mr. Whole=Sum goes to school where he tries his best to do his best. He listens to his teachers and knows a little effort goes along way. Just like he plays hard at soccer, he works hard in school to learn and be successful.

5+0   4+1
3+2   2+3
        1+4

6=

Six, Mr. Whole=Sum adds meditation to his mix.

Meditate; what is that? What does that mean? Meditate means to "think." A natural way to calm down and soothe the mind, body, and soul.

Mr. Whole=Sum spends a little time each day to be mindful and to sit still and quiet to meditate.

Take a deep breath and just relax! There you go! Meditate on that while you just chillax.

6+0   5+1   4+2
3+3   2+4   1+5

7=

Seven, feels like heaven!

Mr. Whole=Sum joins his family in the evening. After a busy day, they love simply spending time together as a family. This is their time to just talk, laugh, and listen to each other share stories about their day.

7+0   6+1   5+2
4+3   3+4   2+5
              1+6

8=

Eight, we cannot be late; we have a date!

Have a date with the bathtub daily! Mr. Whole=Sum is mindful to take a bath or shower in the evening, so he goes to bed so fresh and so clean.

This is part of his hygiene routine.

8+0   7+1   6+2
5+3   4+4   3+5
       2+6   1+7

Nine, we are still feeling fine and divine! Did you know this enchilada has teeth?

Ha! Hilarious, right? Not if he isn't brushing & flossing them twice a day! Mr. Whole=Sum brushes his teeth first thing in the morning and again right before bed. That's why his smile is a thing of beauty!

9+0   6+3   3+6
8+1   5+4   2+7
7+2   4+5   1+8

10=

Ten, is it over or about to begin?

Mr. Whole=Sum was taught to say his prayers and give thanks! He shows gratitude and appreciation for all the things in his beautiful life!

10+0   9+1   8+2

7+3   6+4   5+5

4+6   3+7   2+8

1+9

#10

11=

Eleven, it is just like heaven! That is just two number 1's sitting side by side.

That's where we started on this counting ride. The eleven is for double the love, so let's make a wish. If everything was done with love and respect, then we would have more Whole=Sum Enchiladas than we could even count. What a wonderful world we would live in then. With love, peace, and true happiness!

11+0	10+1	9+2	8+3
7+4	6+5	5+6	4+7
	3+8	2+9	1+10

#11

12=

Twelve! Into sleep we delve! Since you are still counting, we are up to a dozen parts!

By now, you must know this enchilada has stolen our hearts! After his prayers have been said, he gets tucked into bed. This young enchilada needs 9 hours of rest so he can grow big and strong and give his body time to repair and refresh.

12+0	11+1	10+2	9+3
8+4	7+5	6+6	5+7
4+8	3+9	2+10	1+11

#12

13=

Thirteen! What do you mean? This enchilada is already a teen!

He is now the sum of his parts to make him = Mr. Whole=Sum Enchilada!

13+0   12+1   11+2   10+3

9+4   8+5   7+6   6+7

5+8   4+9   3+10   2+11

1+12

Thank you for reading and counting along the parts that equal the Sum to Mr. Whole=Sum Enchilada. Be your own Whole=Sum Enchilada, and follow your dreams and hearts! You can be whatever you want! If you work hard at it and love yourself! True Story!

The End